HARTLEY BEAR™
by Anthony Fletcher

This book is dedicated to our children,
Jordan and Jessica, who were the
inspiration for the characters.

Hartley Bear's Christmas Story

First published 1996 by
Kibworth Books,
Imperial Road,
Kibworth Beauchamp,
Leicestershire,
LE8 0HR.

ISBN 0-7239-0185-6

Printed and bound in Italy.

KIBWORTH
—BOOKS—

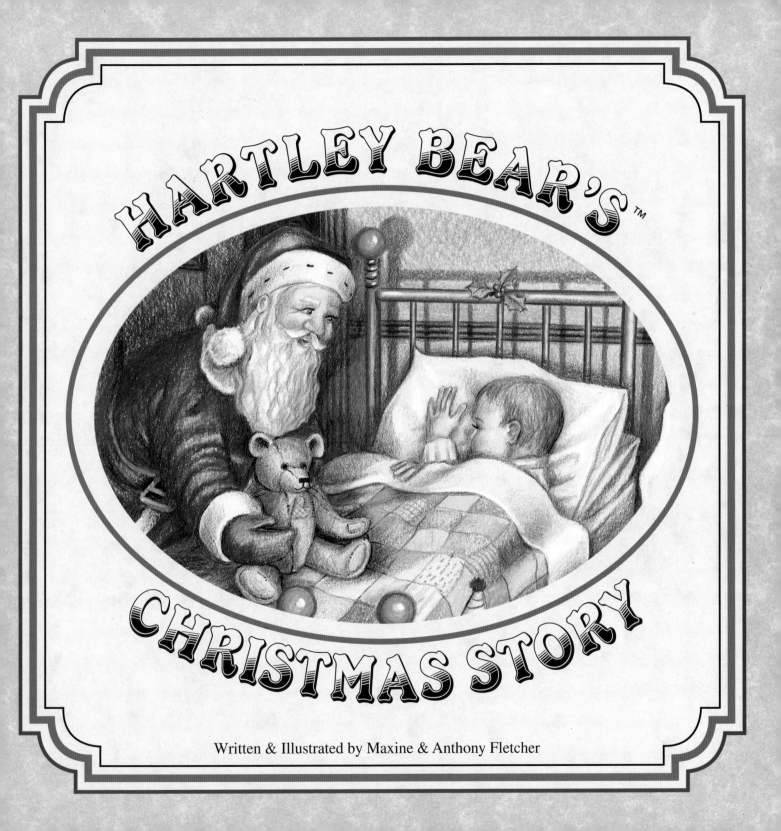

HARTLEY BEAR'S™

CHRISTMAS STORY

Written & Illustrated by Maxine & Anthony Fletcher

It was a cold winter's morning. When James and Emily looked out of the window, they saw that a crisp white blanket of snow had fallen during the night. How lovely it looked!

"Oh, what fun!" squealed Emily, barely able to contain her excitement, "Christmas Eve is here at last, and James, just look at all the pretty snowflakes outside."

James and Emily got washed and dressed and ran downstairs. There was so much to do!

"Let's decorate the tree!" said Mummy.

"Oh, yes," cried the children.

The coloured baubles shone brightly. James and Emily busied themselves making paper chains.

When the last decoration had been put in place, everyone agreed that it was the prettiest Christmas tree ever.

"Let's go for a short walk," suggested Mummy.

Outside it was icy cold. The air was frosty and the snow crunched beneath their feet.

The children chattered excitedly until they came to a very special shop – Mr. Brown's toy shop!

Emily rushed inside leaving James standing next to his mother, gazing longingly at all the wonderful toys in the window. A little teddy sitting on a rocking horse caught his eye.

As James and his mother walked into the shop,

Mr. Brown appeared from his storeroom. He

was an old man with a wrinkled face, grey hair

and spectacles.

"Hello, children," he said. "Can you see anything

you would like Santa Claus to bring you?"

James thought for a while and then asked,

"Please may I have a closer look at the teddy

which is sitting on the rocking horse?"

Mr. Brown reached into the window and handed the bear to James. It had a heart-shaped patch on its chest. James cuddled the bear happily.

"I hope Santa brings me a teddy just like this one," he said.

"You'd have to be a very special little boy to get that bear," said Mr. Brown.

"Why?" asked James.

"Because it's a magic bear," said the old man.

It was nearly bedtime when they got home, but there was still a great deal to do to prepare the house for Santa's visit. Mummy helped James pour a glass of sherry and Emily ran off to the kitchen and came back with a carrot and a mince pie. The children arranged the little feast on a small table and left a message at the side of it. It read: 'To Santa with love.' Then they hung their stockings at the end of their beds.

At last everyone was tucked up in bed asleep. The house was silent except for the ticking of the grandfather clock.

Suddenly, there was a pitter-patter of hooves on the roof. Santa Claus had arrived! Down the chimney he came, his sack bulging at the seams. He brushed the soot off his smart red coat and made his way upstairs to the children's bedroom.

How Santa enjoyed the mince pie and the glass of sherry James and Emily had left for him! He popped the carrot into his pocket to give to the reindeer later. As he filled James' and Emily's stockings, he rummaged around in his sack and pulled out a small teddy bear. It had a heart-shaped patch on its chest. Santa placed the teddy carefully on James' bed. Soon he was on his sleigh, flying across the night sky.

James woke up suddenly. As he rubbed his eyes, he saw a little bear standing on the bed looking down at him.

"Hello James," said the bear. "My name is Hartley, and I'd like to be your friend. Shall we wake your sister?"

Emily was just as amazed as James to see the little bear. The children got out of bed and followed Hartley on tiptoe into the nursery.

Once in the nursery, Hartley introduced the children to his friends, Clown, Toy Soldier, Wooden Doll, Rag Doll and Jack Rabbit.

As the children chattered to the toys, Hartley climbed onto the window-sill and gazed at the white world outside.

"Quickly," he said to the children. "Put on some warm clothes. We're all going outside to play in the snow."

The smaller toys found it very difficult to walk in the snow, especially poor Jack Rabbit. Luckily Hartley spotted James' sledge propped up against the garden shed and the children enjoyed giving each of the toys a ride in turn.

SPLOSH! A snowball hit Clown in the face. Jack Rabbit had started a snowball fight! The children squealed and laughed with delight as they played happily with their new friends.

"Let's build a snowman!" said Hartley.

Everyone set to work and soon they were all admiring the tall, white figure before them.

James ran off to fetch Grandpa's old hat and scarf from the shed to put on the snowman, while Hartley found some pieces of coal for his eyes and a big smiling mouth. The snowman looked splendid, but James still sighed.

"Poor Mr. Snowman hasn't got a nose," he said.

"Perhaps this will do," said a kind voice behind them. To their amazement it was Santa holding the carrot which the children had left for the reindeer. James was so eager to tell Santa all that had happened to them so far, that he put the carrot in his pocket and forgot all about it.

Santa whispered something to Hartley.

"Listen," said Hartley to the children. "Santa would like to take us for a ride on his sleigh."

"Hooray!" they cheered, as they settled down among the sacks of presents. High into the sky flew the reindeer, almost touching the stars! It was a magical ride, but all too soon it was time for Santa to take them home and go back to his work. He still had lots of toys to deliver. The sleigh landed and they said goodbye.

Back in the nursery, everyone seemed a little sad now that the excitement was over.

"Let's have a party," suggested Hartley.

So James and Emily disappeared to the kitchen and came back with cakes, buns and an enormous Christmas pudding. The toys were busy playing a game of hide-and-seek. Hartley peeped around the door and spotted Clown.

"I've seen you!" he shouted, gleefully.

Soon the food was ready and everyone tucked in heartily.

"Shall we play Blind-Man's Buff?" asked Hartley when he had finished. They all agreed. James tied a hanky around Emily's eyes and turned her around three times. Emily stretched her arms out in front of her and tried to catch someone. Soon she stumbled across Clown, who was busy eating Christmas Pudding.

Clown put the blindfold on for his turn.

"Over here," teased Hartley.

Clown set off in the direction of the little bear's voice, but his feet were so big and clumsy in their clown shoes that he fell head over heels and knocked a large flower vase off the table.

It smashed as it hit the ground. Everyone froze as they heard a voice on the landing. The door started to open but then the voice faded away.

"Come on, sleepy heads. It's Christmas Day!" It was Mummy and Daddy calling them. James and Emily squealed with delight as they unwrapped their presents one by one. Who should be inside but their friends from the night before! The children looked at each other and then told Mummy and Daddy all about their adventures with Hartley Bear and his friends. Mummy and Daddy laughed.

James and Emily were disappointed that their parents did not believe their story. Later that morning Daddy looked out of the window and to his surprise saw a very large snowman.

"I think Santa has left you another present, children," he said. James and Emily couldn't believe their eyes! "He still hasn't got a nose," said Emily. James felt in his pocket and there was the carrot Santa had given him!

The children now knew that their adventure had been real. That evening, as James and Emily listened to the carol singers outside in the street, James cuddled Hartley. He knew Santa had given him a very special little bear who had already become a very special friend.

Maybe they would have some more exciting adventures together.

Somehow I think they will, don't you?

ATTACH A

PHOTOGRAPH OF

YOUR SPECIAL

CHRISTMAS

HERE